Little Big Giant

Stories of Wisdom and Inspiration

Introduction

As the final notes of his masterpiece, Symphony No. 9, echoed through the concert hall, Ludwig van Beethoven stood on stage, his face contorted in a mix of exhaustion and triumph. The audience erupted into thunderous applause, but Beethoven couldn't hear it. He had been deaf for years, yet his music spoke louder than any words ever could. This was just one of the many incredible moments in the life of the legendary composer, whose genius and perseverance continue to inspire generations.

Table of Contents

Chapter 1

Early Life and Childhood: Beethoven's

Musical Beginnings

Ludwig van Beethoven was born on December 16, 1770, in Bonn, Germany. He was the second oldest of seven children in his family. His father, Johann, was a musician and taught Beethoven how to play the piano and violin at a very young age. Beethoven's mother, Maria, also played the piano and was a loving and supportive figure in his life.

Even as a young child, Beethoven showed a natural talent for music. He was able to play simple tunes on the piano by the age of four and composed his first piece of music at the age of nine. His father recognized his son's musical abilities and began to give him more formal lessons.

As a child, Beethoven was a quiet and serious boy. He often spent hours practicing the piano and studying music. His family was not wealthy, so Beethoven's father had to work hard to provide for his family. This meant that Beethoven did not have the same opportunities as other children his age. He did not attend school regularly and instead received most of his education at home.

Despite his lack of formal education, Beethoven's love for music continued to grow. He was determined to become a great musician and spent countless hours perfecting his skills. His dedication paid off when he was able to give his first public performance at the age of seven.

Beethoven's musical talents were noticed by the Elector of Cologne, who offered to pay for his education in Vienna, Austria. At the age of 17, Beethoven moved to Vienna to study with some of the best musicians of his time. He was quickly recognized as a musical prodigy and became a sought-after pianist and composer.

Key Takeaway: Beethoven's love for music began at a very young age and he showed a natural talent for it. Despite facing challenges and not having the same opportunities as other children, he remained dedicated to his craft and became one of the greatest composers in history.

Chapter 2

The Influence of His Father and Early

Musical Education

Ludwig van Beethoven was born on December 16, 1770 in Bonn, Germany. His father, Johann van Beethoven, was a musician and taught young Ludwig how to play the piano and violin at a very early age. Johann was a strict and demanding teacher, often pushing his son to practice for hours on end. But this strict upbringing would prove to be crucial in shaping Beethoven's musical talents.

As a child, Beethoven showed a natural talent for music. He was able to play complicated pieces on the piano by ear, without any formal training. His father recognized his son's musical abilities and decided to give him a proper education in music. He arranged for Beethoven to take lessons from the best musicians in Bonn, including the court organist, Christian Gottlob Neefe.

Under Neefe's guidance, Beethoven learned how to read sheet music and play the harpsichord, organ, and viola. He also studied music theory and composition, which allowed him to write his own music. Beethoven's father was very proud of his son's progress and often boasted about him to others. However, this praise and attention also put a lot of pressure on young Beethoven to excel in his musical studies.

Despite the pressure, Beethoven continued to thrive and impress his teachers. By the age of 12, he had already composed his first piece of music, a set of nine variations for piano. His talent was evident to all who heard him play, and it wasn't long before he caught the attention of the Elector of Cologne, who offered to sponsor Beethoven's musical education in Vienna.

At the age of 17, Beethoven left Bonn and traveled to Vienna, where he would spend the rest of his life. He studied under the famous composer Joseph Haydn and quickly gained a reputation as a talented musician. But even in Vienna, Beethoven's father's influence was still present. Johann would often send letters to his son, giving him advice and criticizing his work.

While Beethoven's father may have been strict and demanding, his early musical education was crucial in shaping him into the legendary composer he would become. Without his father's guidance and support, Beethoven may not have had the same level of discipline and determination to succeed in the competitive world of music.

Key Takeaway: The influence of Beethoven's father and his early musical education played a significant role in shaping him into the musical genius he became. His strict upbringing and exposure to different instruments and music theory allowed him to develop his natural talent and become one of the greatest composers of all time.

Chapter 3

Beethoven's Rise to Fame: His First Public

Performances

Ludwig van Beethoven was a young boy with a passion for music. He had been playing the piano since he was just four years old and his talent was undeniable. But it wasn't until he was in his early twenties that he truly began to make a name for himself.

Beethoven's first public performance was at the age of 22, when he played the piano in a concert hall in Vienna, Austria. The audience was amazed by his skills and his ability to play complex pieces with ease. From that moment on, Beethoven's name began to spread throughout the city.

He was soon invited to perform at other concerts and events, and each time, he left the audience in awe. His music was unlike anything they had ever heard before. It was powerful, emotional, and full of passion. People couldn't get enough of it.

As Beethoven's fame grew, so did his confidence. He began to experiment with different styles of music, blending classical and romantic elements to create his own unique sound. This made him stand out even more in the music world.

One of Beethoven's most memorable performances was at a private concert for the royal family. He played his famous piece, "Moonlight Sonata," and it was said that even the Queen was moved to tears. From that moment on, Beethoven was no longer just a local sensation, but a national one.

But with fame also came criticism. Some people didn't understand Beethoven's music and thought it was too unconventional. They even called him "mad" because of his intense dedication to his work. But Beethoven didn't let their words bring him down. He continued to compose and perform, pushing the boundaries of music and inspiring others to do the same.

Key Takeaway: Beethoven's first public performances were the beginning of his rise to fame. Despite facing criticism, he stayed true to his unique style and became one of the most influential composers of all time. This teaches us to embrace our individuality and not be afraid to be different.

Chapter 4

The Creation of His Most Famous Works:

Symphony No. 5 and Moonlight Sonata

Ludwig van Beethoven had already established himself as a brilliant composer, but he was about to create two of his most famous works that would solidify his place in music history. These were Symphony No. 5 and Moonlight Sonata.

Symphony No. 5, also known as the "Fate Symphony," was composed between 1804 and 1808. It is one of the most

recognizable and beloved pieces of
classical music, with its iconic four-note
opening motif. But the journey to its
creation was not an easy one for
Beethoven.

At the time, Beethoven was struggling
with his hearing loss, which was getting
worse by the day. He was also dealing with
personal and financial troubles. But despite
all of this, he poured his heart and soul
into Symphony No. 5. He spent years
perfecting every note and every melody,
determined to create a masterpiece that
would stand the test of time.

Finally, in December of 1808, Symphony No. 5 had its premiere in Vienna. The audience was in awe of Beethoven's genius, and the symphony received a standing ovation. It was a triumphant moment for Beethoven, who had overcome so many obstacles to create this magnificent piece of music.

Moonlight Sonata, also known as Piano Sonata No. 14, was composed in 1801. It is a beautiful and haunting piece that showcases Beethoven's mastery of the piano. The first movement, known as "Adagio sostenuto," is often described as a "moonlit landscape" due to its dreamy and melancholic melody.

But Moonlight Sonata was not initially well-received. Some critics thought it was too unconventional and too emotional. However, over time, it gained popularity and is now considered one of Beethoven's greatest works.

Beethoven's dedication to his craft and his determination to create something extraordinary, even in the face of adversity, is evident in both Symphony No. 5 and Moonlight Sonata. These works have stood the test of time and continue to inspire and move people of all ages.

Key Takeaway: Even when faced with challenges, never give up on your dreams and passions. Beethoven's perseverance and dedication to his music resulted in two timeless masterpieces that continue to be admired and loved by people all over the world.

Chapter 5

Dealing with Hearing Loss: Beethoven's

Struggle and Adaptation

Ludwig van Beethoven was a musical genius. His fingers flew across the piano keys, creating beautiful melodies that left audiences in awe. But as he grew older, Beethoven faced a challenge that threatened to silence his music forever - hearing loss.

It started with a ringing in his ears, but soon Beethoven noticed that he couldn't hear certain notes as clearly as he used to. As a composer and musician, this was devastating news. Music was his passion, his purpose, and without his hearing, he feared he would never be able to create the same beautiful sounds again.

But Beethoven refused to let his hearing loss defeat him. He adapted and found new ways to continue making music. He would place a wooden rod between his teeth and press it against the piano, allowing him to feel the vibrations of the notes. This helped him to continue composing and performing, even as his hearing continued to decline.

Despite his struggles, Beethoven's music continued to amaze and inspire. He composed some of his most famous works, such as the Ninth Symphony and the Moonlight Sonata, while completely deaf. He even conducted orchestras by feeling the vibrations of the music through a special rod attached to the floor.

Beethoven's hearing loss was a constant battle for him, but he never let it stop him from pursuing his passion. He found new ways to adapt and continue creating beautiful music, inspiring others to never give up on their dreams.

Key Takeaway: Beethoven's story teaches us the importance of perseverance and determination. No matter what challenges we may face, we can find ways to adapt and continue pursuing our passions.

Chapter 6

The Immortal Beloved: Beethoven's Love

Life and Relationships

Ludwig van Beethoven was known for his incredible talent as a composer, but his personal life was just as intriguing. Despite his deafness, Beethoven was a passionate and romantic man who had his fair share of love and heartbreak. In this chapter, we will explore Beethoven's love life and the mysterious figure known as his "Immortal Beloved."

Beethoven had many romantic relationships throughout his life, but the most significant one was with a woman who remains a mystery to this day. In 1812, Beethoven wrote a passionate love letter to an unknown woman, referring to her as his "Immortal Beloved." The letter was never sent, and it was only discovered after his death. This has led to much speculation and mystery surrounding the identity of this woman.

Some believe that the Immortal Beloved was Antonie Brentano, a married woman whom Beethoven had a close relationship with. Others suggest it was Beethoven's student, Julie Guicciardi, whom he dedicated his famous "Moonlight Sonata" to. However, there is no concrete evidence to support these theories.

Despite the mystery surrounding the Immortal Beloved, one thing is for sure – Beethoven was deeply in love with her. In his letter, he expressed his longing for her and his desire to be with her. He wrote, "My heart is full of so many things to say to you – ah – there are moments when I feel that speech amounts to nothing at all."

Unfortunately, Beethoven's love for the Immortal Beloved was not meant to be. She never responded to his letter, and the two never had a chance to be together. Some believe that she may have been married or that Beethoven's deafness made it challenging for them to communicate.

Aside from the Immortal Beloved, Beethoven had other significant relationships in his life. He was briefly engaged to Therese Malfatti, but the engagement was broken off due to her family's disapproval. He also had a close relationship with his nephew, Karl, whom he took in after his brother's death.

However, Beethoven's love life was not without its share of heartbreak. He had a difficult relationship with his mother, who was an alcoholic and passed away when he was only 16 years old. He also had a strained relationship with his father, who was known for his strictness and often disapproved of Beethoven's career as a musician.

Key Takeaway: Despite his deafness, Beethoven was a passionate and romantic man who had his fair share of love and heartbreak. His mysterious love for the Immortal Beloved remains a topic of fascination to this day, showcasing the depth of Beethoven's emotions and his longing for love and companionship.

Chapter 7

The Napoleon Incident: Beethoven's Political Views and Impact on His Music

Ludwig van Beethoven was a man of many talents. He was a brilliant composer, a skilled pianist, and a passionate lover of music. But did you know that he was also a man with strong political views? In this chapter, we will explore how Beethoven's political beliefs influenced his music and how one particular incident changed the course of his career.

Beethoven was born in Bonn, Germany in 1770. At that time, Germany was not a unified country, but a collection of small states ruled by different princes and kings. Beethoven's father, Johann, was a court musician for the Elector of Cologne, a powerful ruler in Germany. From a young age, Beethoven was exposed to the politics of the court and was often surrounded by discussions of power and authority.

As Beethoven grew older, he became more and more interested in politics. He believed in the ideals of the French Revolution, which called for liberty, equality, and fraternity. He saw the revolution as a way to overthrow the old, corrupt rulers and create a better society for all people. Beethoven's political views were reflected in his music, which often had a sense of rebellion and defiance.

But it was one particular incident that solidified Beethoven's political stance and had a significant impact on his music. In 1804, Napoleon Bonaparte declared himself Emperor of France, going against the ideals of the French Revolution. Beethoven, who had initially admired Napoleon for his revolutionary ideas, was deeply disappointed and angered by this turn of events.

In a fit of rage, Beethoven took the title of his latest symphony, Symphony No. 3, "Eroica," which means "heroic," and dedicated it to Napoleon. He saw Napoleon as a hero who would bring freedom and equality to the people. However, when he heard that Napoleon had declared himself Emperor, Beethoven scratched out the dedication and changed the title to "Sinfonia Eroica, composta per festeggiare il sovvenire di un grande uomo" (Heroic

Symphony, composed to celebrate the memory of a great man).

This incident not only showed Beethoven's strong political beliefs but also marked a shift in his music. His symphonies became more complex and dramatic, reflecting the turmoil and conflict of the political landscape. He also started incorporating themes of heroism and struggle in his music, inspired by the ideals of the French Revolution.

Key Takeaway: Beethoven's political views and the Napoleon incident had a profound impact on his music. It not only shaped his compositions but also showed how music can be a powerful tool for expressing one's beliefs and emotions. Beethoven's story teaches us to stand up for what we believe in and use our talents to make a difference in the world.

Chapter 8

The Late Years: Beethoven's Final Works

and Legacy

As Beethoven entered his late years, he faced many challenges. His hearing continued to deteriorate, making it difficult for him to communicate with others and even compose music. Despite these obstacles, Beethoven persevered and created some of his most famous and powerful works.

One of Beethoven's most well-known pieces from this time was his Ninth Symphony, which included a choir singing the famous "Ode to Joy" melody. This was the first time a choir was used in a symphony, and it was a groundbreaking moment in music history. Beethoven's Ninth Symphony is still performed and loved by people all over the world today.

Another notable work from this period was his Missa Solemnis, a religious mass that took Beethoven over four years to complete. This piece was a testament to Beethoven's deep faith and his dedication to creating music that was both beautiful and meaningful.

Despite his struggles with his health, Beethoven continued to push the boundaries of music. He experimented with different forms and techniques, creating works that were both complex and emotional. One example of this is his late string quartets, which are considered some of the most profound and challenging pieces of music ever written.

Beethoven's legacy continued to grow even after his death. His music inspired countless composers and musicians, and his impact on the world of music is immeasurable. Today, his works are still studied and performed, and his name is synonymous with greatness in the world of classical music.

Key Takeaway: Even in the face of challenges and obstacles, Beethoven's determination and passion for music never wavered. His late works are a testament to his genius and his legacy continues to inspire generations of musicians.

Chapter 9

Beethoven's Musical Style: Breaking the

Rules and Revolutionizing Music

Ludwig van Beethoven was not your average composer. He didn't follow the rules of music like everyone else. In fact, he broke them and created his own unique style that would change the world of music forever.

Beethoven was a rebel at heart. He didn't like being told what to do, especially when it came to his music. He believed that music should come from the heart and soul, not from a set of strict rules. This mindset led him to create some of the most powerful and emotional pieces of music the world has ever heard.

One of the ways Beethoven broke the rules was by using unexpected harmonies and chords in his compositions. In the past, composers followed specific guidelines on which chords and notes should be used in a piece of music. But Beethoven didn't care about those rules. He experimented with different combinations of notes, creating a sound that was completely his own.

Another way Beethoven revolutionized music was through his use of dynamics. Dynamics refer to the volume of the music, and Beethoven was a master at using them to convey emotion. He would often start a piece softly and then suddenly increase the volume, creating a dramatic effect. This was unheard of at the time, but Beethoven didn't care. He wanted to express his emotions through his music, and he did it in a way that captivated his audience.

Beethoven also challenged the traditional structure of music. In the past, composers followed a specific form when writing a piece of music. But Beethoven didn't like to be confined to a structure. He would often change the order of sections or add new ones, creating a sense of unpredictability in his music. This made his compositions exciting and kept his listeners on the edge of their seats.

But perhaps the most significant way Beethoven broke the rules was through his use of instruments. He was one of the first composers to incorporate instruments like the trombone and piccolo into his symphonies. He also used instruments in unconventional ways, such as using the cello as a solo instrument, which was not common at the time. This expanded the possibilities of what could be done with music and paved the way for future composers to experiment with different instruments and sounds.

Key Takeaway: Beethoven's musical style was all about breaking the rules and creating something new and unique. He didn't follow the traditional guidelines of music, but instead, he let his emotions guide him. By doing so, he revolutionized the world of music and inspired future generations of composers to think outside the box and push the boundaries of what was considered "normal."

Chapter 10

The Legacy of Ludwig van Beethoven: His Influence on Music and the World Today

Ludwig van Beethoven was not just a talented musician, but a true genius who changed the course of music forever. His legacy continues to live on, even centuries after his death. Let's explore how Beethoven's influence can still be felt in the world today.

Beethoven's Music

Beethoven's music is timeless and has stood the test of time. His compositions are still widely performed and enjoyed by people all over the world. His most famous works, such as "Moonlight Sonata" and "Symphony No. 5", are recognized by people of all ages. Beethoven's music is not just limited to classical music, but has also been incorporated into other genres such as pop, rock, and even rap. His influence can be heard in the music of many modern artists, showing that his legacy is still alive and well.

Breaking the Rules

Beethoven was known for breaking the traditional rules of music and creating his own unique style. He was not afraid to experiment and push the boundaries, which is why his music is so revolutionary. Beethoven's boldness and innovation inspired other composers to do the same, leading to the development of new styles and techniques in music. Even today, musicians are encouraged to think outside the box and break the rules, just like Beethoven did.

Inspiring Future Generations

Beethoven's music has been inspiring future generations of musicians for centuries. Many famous composers, such as Brahms and Tchaikovsky, were influenced by Beethoven's works and incorporated elements of his style into their own compositions. Even modern-day musicians continue to be inspired by Beethoven's music, proving that his legacy is still relevant and influential.

A Symbol of Perseverance

Beethoven's life was not easy. He faced many challenges, including losing his hearing at a young age. Despite these obstacles, he continued to create beautiful music and never gave up. Beethoven's determination and perseverance serve as a reminder to us all that anything is possible if we work hard and never give up. He is a true inspiration and his legacy serves as a symbol of hope and determination.

Key Takeaway

Ludwig van Beethoven's legacy is still very much alive in the world today. His music continues to be enjoyed and his influence can be seen in the works of many modern artists. Beethoven's boldness, innovation, and perseverance serve as an inspiration to future generations, encouraging them to break the rules and create their own unique path. Beethoven's legacy will continue to live on and inspire people for generations to come.

Dear Reader,

Thank you for choosing "Little Big Giant - Stories of Wisdom and Inspiration"! We hope this book has inspired and motivated you on your own journey to success.

If you enjoyed reading this book and believe in the power of its message, we kindly ask for your support. Please consider leaving a positive review on the platform where you purchased the book. Your review will help spread the message to more young readers, empowering them to dream big and achieve greatness. We acknowledge that mistakes can happen, and we appreciate your forgiveness.

Remember, the overall message of this book is the key. Thank you for being a part of our mission to inspire and uplift young minds.

Made in United States
Orlando, FL
18 December 2024

56021216R00049